A Hen, A Chick and A String Guitar

For Richard Scholtz; I dance every time he plays! — M. R. M.
To my friend Serge — S. F.

Barefoot Books
2067 Massachusetts Ave
Cambridge, MA 02140

Text copyright © 2005 by Margaret Read MacDonald
Illustrations copyright © 2005 by Sophie Fatus
The moral right of Margaret Read MacDonald to be identified as the author and Sophie Fatus
to be identified as the illustrator of this work has been asserted

First published in the United States of America in 2005 by Barefoot Books Inc

This book was typeset in Bembo Schoolbook 29 on 37 point and Cerigo Bold 36 point
The illustrations were prepared in acrylics and pastels
Graphic design by Judy Linard. Color separation by Bright Arts Singapore
Printed and bound in Hong Kong by South China Printing Co.
This book has been printed on 100% acid-free paper

Library of Congress Cataloging-in-Publication Data
MacDonald, Margaret Read, 1940-
  A hen, a chick, and a string guitar / retold by Margaret Read MacDonald ; illustrated by Sophie Fatus.
    p. cm.
  Summary: A cumulative tale from Chile that begins with a hen and ends with sixteen different animals
and a guitar.
  ISBN 1-84148-796-1 (alk. paper)
  [1. Folklore--Chile.] I. Fatus, Sophie, ill. II. Title.
  PZ8.1.M15924Iah 2005
  398.2'0983'0452--dc22
  2004017830

1 3 5 7 9 8 6 4 2

A Hen, A Chick and A String Guitar

Inspired by a Chilean folk tale

written by Margaret Read MacDonald

illustrated by Sophie Fatus

Barefoot Books
Celebrating Art and Story

Grandpa gave me a clucking red hen.

"Cluck! Cluck! Cluck! Cluck!"

Ay! Ay! Ay! What a fine hen!

"Cluck! Cluck! Cluck! Cluck!"

One day that hen

Gave me a chick.

I had a hen,

And I had a chick.

Ay! Ay! Ay! Ay!

How I loved my two little pets!

Grandma gave me a quacking white duck.

"Quack! Quack! Quack!
Quack! Quack! Quack!"

Ay! Ay! Ay! What a fine duck!
"Quack! Quack! Quack! Quack!"
One day that duck
Gave me a duckling.

I had a duck,
And I had a duckling.
I had a hen,
I had a chick.

Ay! Ay! Ay! Ay!
How I loved my four little pets!

Uncle gave me a purring yellow cat.

"Purr! Purr! Purr!"

Ay! Ay! Ay! What a fine cat!
"Purr! Purr! Purr!"
One day that cat
Gave me a kitten.

I had a cat,
And I had a kitten.
I had a duck.
I had a duckling.
I had a hen.
I had a chick.

Ay! Ay! Ay! Ay!
How I loved my six little pets!

Auntie gave me a barking black dog.

"Ay! Ay! Ay! What a fine dog!
"Woof! Woof! Woof! Woof! Woof!"

"Woof! Woof! Woof! Woof! Woof! Woof! Woof!"

One day that dog
Gave me a puppy.

I had a dog,
And I had a puppy.
I had a cat.
I had a kitten.
I had a duck.
I had a duckling.
I had a hen.
I had a chick.

Ay! Ay! Ay! Ay!
How I loved my eight little pets!

Brother gave me a bleating white sheep.

"Baa! Baa! Baa!"

Ay! Ay! Ay! What a fine sheep!
"Baa! Baa! Baa!"

One day that sheep
Gave me a lamb.

I had a sheep,
And I had a lamb.
A dog…a puppy.
A cat…a kitten.
A duck…a duckling.
A hen…a chick.

Ay! Ay! Ay! Ay!
How I loved my
ten little pets!

Sister gave me an oinking pink pig.

"Oink! Oink! Oink! Oink! Oink!"

Ay! Ay! Ay! What a fine pig!
"Oink! Oink! Oink! Oink!"

One day that pig
Gave me a piglet.

I had a pig,
And I had a piglet.
A sheep…a lamb.
A dog…a puppy.
A cat…a kitten.
A duck…a duckling.
I had a hen.
I had a chick.

Ay! Ay! Ay! Ay!
How I loved my twelve little pets!

Mother gave me a mooing brown cow.

"Moo! Moo! Moo!"

Ay! Ay! Ay! What a fine cow!
"Moo! Moo! Moo!"
One day that cow
Gave me a calf.

I had a cow,
And I had a calf.
A pig…a piglet.
A sheep…a lamb.
A dog…a puppy.
A cat…a kitten.
A duck…a duckling.
A hen…a chick.

Ay! Ay! Ay! Ay!
How I loved my fourteen pets!

Father gave me a neighing gray horse.

"Neigh! Neigh! Neigh!"

Ay! Ay! Ay! What a fine horse!
"Neigh! Neigh! Neigh!"
One day that horse
Gave me a colt.

A sheep...a lamb!

A pig...a piglet!

A cow...a calf!

I had a horse,
And I had a colt.

A dog...a puppy!

A cat...a kitten!

A duck...a duckling!

I had a hen,
And I had a chick.

Ay! Ay! Ay! Ay!
How I loved my sixteen pets!

My friend gave me a little guitar!

"Plunk! Plunk!

Plunk! Plunk! Plunk!

Ay! Ay! Ay! What a fine guitar!

"Plunk! Plunk! Plunk! Plunk! Plunk!"

Plunk!"

And every time I played my guitar
My pets all came from near and far...

The horse danced
And the colt danced!

The cow danced
And the calf danced!

The pig danced
And the piglet danced!

The sheep danced
And the lamb danced!

The dog danced
And the puppy danced!

The cat danced
And the kitten danced!

The duck danced
And the duckling danced!

The hen danced
And the chick danced!

They all danced
And I danced too!

Ay! Ay! Ay! Ay!
How I love all of my pets!

SOURCES

This story was inspired by *Folklore Chileno* by Oreste Plath (Santiago: Nascimento, 1969). A similar text is found in *Folklore Portorriqueño* by Rafael Ramirez de Arellano (Madrid: Centro de Estudios Históricos, 1926). The tale appears as a folk song in *Folktales of Mexico* by Americo Paredes (University of Chicago Press, 1970). Chilean storyteller Carlos Genovese informs me that versions of this tale are told throughout Chile and Latin America. Usually the child has a "real y media" coin and begins buying animals. For this picture book, liberties have been taken with the tale to create a playful children's version in English. The Chilean version gave no music, so the musicians created the song on the accompanying disc. The tale seems to appear as a folk song in some areas and as a simple told story in others. The artist has chosen to illustrate the story with an Andean setting. The Aymara live in the north-easternmost corner of Chile.

For a guitar score to accompany this book, please visit our website.

Barefoot Books
Celebrating Art and Story

At Barefoot Books, we celebrate art and story with books that open the hearts and minds of children from all walks of life, inspiring them to read deeper, search further, and explore their own creative gifts. Taking our inspiration from many different cultures, we focus on themes that encourage independence of spirit, enthusiasm for learning, and acceptance of other traditions. Thoughtfully prepared by writers, artists, and storytellers from all over the world, our products combine the best of the present with the best of the past to educate our children as the caretakers of tomorrow.

www.barefootbooks.com